PUKEY POETRY

Tale Ticklers by Mz Millipede

With love n' laughter!

PUKEY POETRY

Tale Ticklers by Mz Millipede

Written and illustrated by Dorianne Allister Winkler

Dedication

Without my mother Mona, (whose unending encouragement and belief in my artistic pursuits kept me going through the years), this book would not have come about. My gratitude to you is eternal. And without my husband's patience and steadfast support on all levels—(not to mention the long hours of editing skills), I could never have finished. To all my friends and family, (you know who you are)—thank you for the constant encouragement when I was ready to call it quits. I am forever grateful.

Mz Millipede Publishing LLC

ISBN: 978-0-9988128-0-9

Pukey Poetry – Tale Ticklers by Mz Millipede.
Text and Illustration copyright © 2017
By Dorianne Allister Winkler. All rights reserved.

Book layout by eBook DesignWorks

Welcome!

Mz Millipede will make you squirm
With tales so strange you will confirm
That nowhere have you ever read
Such stories filled with mirth and dread!

She's not your average millipede,
She likes to shrink down small
And change her color frequently
Or suddenly grow tall.

Her house is warm and friendly,
It is where she spends her time
Painting in the art room and
Writing tales that rhyme.

You'll find her in each story
Sometimes hiding—sometimes not—
She knows you'll like these tale ticklers,
She'll make you laugh a lot.

So hold onto your chuckling belly
Before you're turned into toad jelly,
Before you're cooked in a cricket stew,
Or a baby monster wants only YOU!
Turn the page on a millipede's dare
You'll find her hiding everywhere.

Lollipop Preeta

Round and purple, red and yellow,
Swirls of pink and blue,
A lollipop so big
I think it weighs much more than you!

It's Lucky Preeta's lollipop,
And she lives down the street,
She'll never say a word to us
She'll only lick and eat.

Her rainbow tongue is miles long
And moves with lightning speed,
It wraps around that lollipop
Without a moment's heed.

I think she has to finish it
Before she's called inside,
'Cause dinnertime is coming up
That pop's too big to hide.

"We can help you if you like—
You're looking rather sickly,
With two of us plus one of you
We can finish quickly!"

Preeta's face turned fire red,
She stopped and looked right at us,
Then stuck her long tongue out and SLURP
She swallowed my friend Gladys!

Toe-Jam Sam

There is a man named Toe-Jam Sam
Who lives behind our school,
He never cuts his fingernails
Or toenails as a rule.
He never ever takes a bath,
He never cuts his hair,
He mostly eats potato chips
And crumbs are everywhere!

I'm thinkin' that when I grow up
I'd like to live like Sam,
'Cause no one tells him what to do
He won't say, "Thank-you Ma'am!"
No one yells at Toe-Jam Sam
Or says, "You have to eat!"
No one makes him change his socks
Since all he wears are feet.

I wish I could meet Toe-Jam Sam,
I'd make him my best friend—
As long as every light stayed on—
And it was all pretend.

Candice Cotta's Cotton Candy

Candice Cotta's cotton candy
Cannot possibly compete
With Carolina's creamy custard
Cooked with crunchy cockroach feet!

So Candice Cotta quickly caught
And cooked a cricket stew,
That chirped and creaked so loudly
Her competition couldn't chew.

O'l Steg

There is a Stegosaurus
Who's living on my street,
'Belongs to my friend Timothy
And boy can ol' Steg eat!
For breakfast, lunch and dinner,
He'll woof down a baseball field,
And anything in sight that's green
He'll gulp it whole or peeled.
So that is why St. Patrick's day
Is scary around here—
Anyone who's wearing green—
Will likely disappear!

Bugs

Chocolate beetles
Peppermint fleas
A caramel grasshopper
Lime honeybees,
Licorice spiders
Wild cherry ants
Cinnamon weevils
Stuck to your pants
Marshmallow ticks
And peanut butter worms
A huge toffee cockroach
Sure to make you squirm

A diet of bugs
Could really be yummy—
However, it might not
Be great for your tummy!

Millipedes do not taste good! ☹

Hippo Cloud

A huge and happy hippo's hovering
Half way in the sky—
A hairless hefty hippo
Hankering helplessly close by.
A hovering hippopotomus—
A hazard overhead!
I wish I had a happy hairy
Hamster cloud instead!

Bloated Toaded

I swallowed fifty flies today
One hundred flying ants
Sixty noisy crickets and
Some very tasty plants.
Grubs and slugs and juicy worms
I stuffed into my belly,
Until a voice behind me said
"I'd love some fresh toad jelly!"

Skink the Skouse

Skink the Skouse
Lives under my house,
He's my very best friend,
All black and white
With a long bushy tail
That he loves me to brush without end.

Skink is polite
He NEVER would bite
Which comes as no surprise.
If he wishes to speak
He will let out a squeak
And look up with his cute beady eyes.

Half skunk—half mouse,
My Skink the Skouse
I treat with the utmost respect—
For if I slip up and his feelings get hurt
There's a smell I can never forget!

Where's Ben?

Every night before going to bed
Ben put a paper bag over his head.
He didn't move or make a sound,
Did anyone know he was around?

His bedroom door opened a little and then
He heard someone whisper, "Have you seen Ben?"
He snickered and giggled and slapped his knee—
Now tell me, how silly can everyone be!

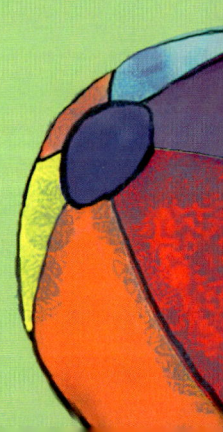

Wafflerus or Pandacake?

I found him in my kitchen
And I could not help but stare
At the waffle eating walrus
Sitting upright in my chair!
He was whoofing down hot waffles
Topped with syrup and whipped cream,
His long teeth stained with blueberries
His whiskers singed from steam.
A Wafflerus they call him,
And you'll find him anywhere
There are Sunday morning waffle smells
Wafting through the air...

So I switched to Sunday pancakes
Hoping then I'd dine alone—
But along came a Pandacake
Who has made my house his own!

The Sad Story of Alice

Alice had a dot
On her skinny chinny chin,
And every day it grew an inch
From somewhere deep within!
It grew and grew until at last
It covered her whole face—
It covered up her arms and legs—
It covered every space!
And so it's said, she disappeared
And no one even missed her!
So pay attention to the things
That start out as a blister.

Latrina Laffayet

When Latrina Laffayet
Takes her Loris to the vet
All the dogs will howl and fret!
Grownups turn around and glare
While their children stop and stare—
Cats puff up beneath their chair
As flying hairs land everywhere!

Yet the animal doc never blinks,
'Cause he knows how this ostrich thinks!
He treats her possums, skunks and minks,
Her boa and her piglet pink.
Sugar glider and wallaby pet,
Tattooed lion and lovebird set...
Yet asked which one he can't forget—

He'll say Latrina Laffayet!

Brother-Monster

Brother-Monster's in our house
He's small with a huge head,
Two round eyes and painted toes,
He only wants MY bed!

When he opens up his mouth
The room begins to shake,
Howls rock the rafters
It's a Brother-Monster quake!

Mom yells, "Just go back to sleep!"
But what's a kid to do,
If Brother-Monster's in your room
And all he wants is YOU!

A Secret Feast

All the bugs came out tonight

To have a secret feast,

While we slept in dream's delight

They marched in from the east.

Covered counters, shelves and chairs

Hundreds

      more

          crept

              down

                  the

                      stairs.

The kitchen floor was covered black

In one gigantic bug attack!

The bugs crawled fast from far

And W I D E

Some marched alone

Some SIDEbySIDE,

And all because of one mistake—

I left out the chocolate cake!

Froogley Man

You say you've seen the Froogley Man
Who hides under your bed?
He comes alive when the lights go out
And growls unless he's fed?
Well, leave him cookies, juice and milk,
Or chips from your backpack—
Maybe sing some spooky songs
In hopes he won't come back!
But, every night at bedtime
When you crawl beneath your sheet—
Look out for that Froogley man
He loves to eat kid's feet!

Bling Bling Bling

Bling bling bling
Mariah just bought a new ring,
She also bought bangles
Jingles and jangles
With 10 rainbow beads on a string.

Bling bling bling
Mariah the jewel queen that gleams,
With glitters and twinkles
Diamonds and sprinkles
She captures our hearts with her dreams.

SLURP-A-DURP!
shlurp
SLUUUURP!
slurrrp!
SLURP!
SLURP
What a train wreck!
SLURRRRRP!

Gaggleburps

Gaggleburps! The alien race
Hang green spaghetti from their face—
They swallow meals in a nano-second
When their hungry stomach's beckon!
Gaggleburps spit out their carrots
Talking fast like hungry parrots
Smashing peas until its goop
Blowing bubbles in their soup—
These Gaggleburps forever scream
When dinner brings them no ice cream
And with a finger in each ear
They make the "should nots" disappear.

I'm proud my food I'll never slurp
So no one calls me GAGGLEBURP!

The Green-Eyed Giant

Once I had a little plant
That grew and Grew and G R E W
Until one day it measured high
Like six foot Uncle Drew!
Its' branches wrapped around my bed
And I could hardly see—
For what had been a tiny plant
Was now a giant tree.

Then one night I climbed in bed
And thought I saw an eye?
A nose—an ear—a tooth and then
I heard it cry—
"Sonny boy", a loud voice said,
"I'm hungry don't ya know.
I'm needin' more than water "
And his eye began to glow.
I thought this over quickly

Pretty please turn the page!

It didn't take too long,
"How about a sandwich," I said,
"That will make you strong!
With peanut butter and strawberry jam
I'll spread it on real thick,
And anything that you could want
I will make it QUICK!"

The giant rolled his green-egg eye,
Then let out a grumble
"Well, gimme one – no, gimme two!"
I heard his tummy rumble!
I left my room, I left my house.
I took a rocket to the moon!
'Cause no green plants grow way up there
Not now, not any time soon.

I'm taking a bite before we lift off...

Strange New Kid

"Will you come over to my house and play?"
A new kid at school asked me today.
"I've got a back yard we can explore
With things you've NEVER seen before—
Like a one eye'd girl who floats on air
And a tribe of aliens with long metal hair.
I once saw a super ginormous croc
Who loves to run after the kids on our block—
And if I am quiet and hideout in my tree,
There are ghosts with black claws who come after me, and…"
"STOP!" I said as I backed away,
"I think I am very busy today,
 There's homework and chores I still have to do,
 So don't call me—I'll call you."

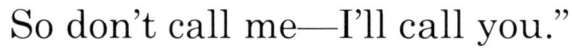

THE END

For more chuckles
follow Mz Milli's "DAILY DIARY"
at PukeyPoetry.com

Dorianne Allister Winkler lives tucked away on the rainbow island of Kauai where she has raised one daughter, eleven cats, a cockatiel, a basenji dog and a husband.

Living in the tropics, she is no stranger to the creepy crawlers that she has learned to share an art studio with—from giant geckos and flying cockroaches, to prehistoric cane spiders and

centipedes. It is not surprising that she authored a book about a magical millipede who illustrates and writes poetry.

As most of her eager enthusiasts are under four feet tall, Dorianne's first book *Mz Millipede's PUKEY POETRY* is written to each and every one of them, with love, laughter and a creepy crawly touch.

CPSIA information can be obtained
at www.ICGtesting.com
Printed in the USA
BVXC01n1120121117
499940BV00001B/1